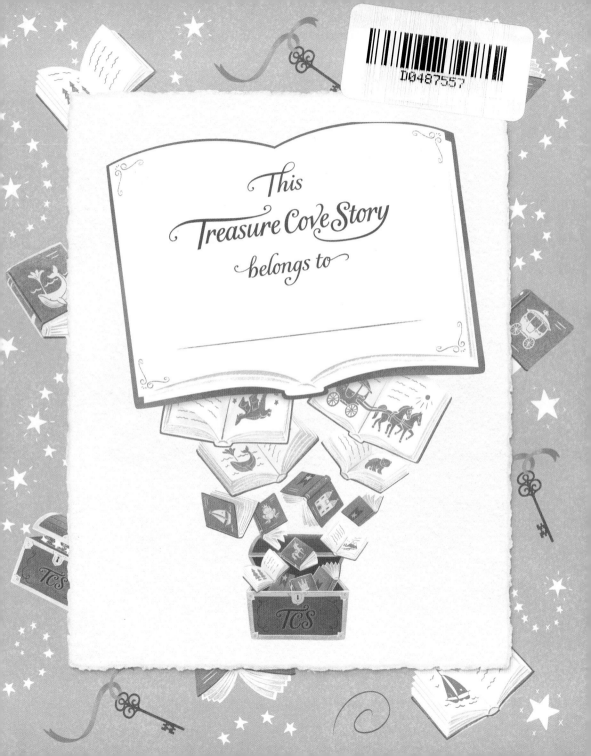

This

Treasure Cove Story

belongs to

HOW TO TRAIN YOUR DRAGON

A CENTUM BOOK 978-1-912396-44-3
Published in Great Britain by Centum Books Ltd.
This edition published 2018.

3 5 7 9 10 8 6 4 2

How To Train Your Dragon © 2018 DreamWorks Animation LLC.
All Rights Reserved.

Centum Books Ltd, 20 Devon Square, Newton Abbot,
Devon, TQ12 2HR, UK.

www.centumbooksltd.co.uk | books@centumbooksltd.co.uk
CENTUM BOOKS Limited Reg.No. 07641486.

A CIP catalogue record for this book is available
from the British Library.

Printed in China.

centum

A Treasure Cove Story

DREAMWORKS
HOW TO TRAIN YOUR
DRAGON

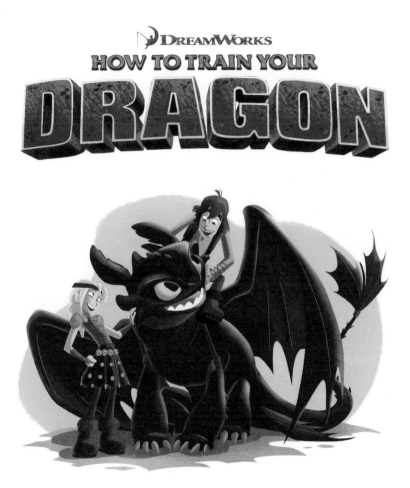

Written by Devra Newberger Speregen
Illustrated by Denise Shimabukuro and Shawn Finley

Long ago, on a faraway island, fire-breathing dragons swooped down into the bustling village of Berk to steal food from the Vikings. And every night the Vikings tried to stop them.

But one Viking boy known as Hiccup was not allowed to fight dragons. Instead, his father put him to work in the village blacksmith shop.

Hiccup's father, Stoick, was the fearless leader of the Vikings. Hiccup begged his father to let him fight dragons alongside other kids.

But Stoick always said no. 'You're too kindhearted and gentle to fight,' he replied.

Now, Hiccup believed that if he could fight a dragon on his own, everybody would see that he was brave and strong.

One night, Hiccup made up his mind. He would sneak out and fight the dragons by himself!

Taking the Mangler – his new dragon-catching invention – Hiccup sneaked out of the shop. He found a spot outside the village, high up on a cliff, where he waited.

Suddenly, something zoomed by Hiccup's head.
He could not see if it was a Gronckle or a Zippleback – but
whatever it was, it was fast and furious! Hiccup aimed the
Mangler and fired into the darkness. Then he heard a loud
ROOOAAAARRRR!

Hiccup's eyes grew big. 'I think I got him!' he cried.

But there was no time to celebrate. Another dragon
started chasing Hiccup through the village! Just before
the dragon could get him, Stoick appeared and chased
it away. Unfortunately, Hiccup had let all the other
dragons accidentally get away, too. His father was furious.
A Viking boy pointed at Hiccup and laughed.
'I've never seen anyone mess up so badly!'

The next day, Hiccup found the dragon
caught in his Mangler's net.

'Wow,' Hiccup said. 'I really did it!
And it's a Night Fury!'

Then he saw that the dragon's tail was broken.
It was all his fault! Hiccup felt so bad that he cut
the poor dragon loose.

The mighty beast leaped up and knocked
Hiccup to the ground! Hiccup was really
scared, but the dragon just turned
and ran away.

At home, Hiccup thought about the Night Fury. He wondered why the dragon had not hurt him. Maybe all the bad things he had heard about dragons were not true.

Hiccup went to tell his father that he did not want to fight anymore. Unfortunately, it was too late. 'You are going to the Dragon Training Academy,' Stoick said.

Dragon Training Academy was a disaster. Astrid, a brave Viking girl, and the other kids made fun of Hiccup when he ran away from a Gronckle. Gobber, their teacher, had to step in and save him. That made the kids laugh even more.

Hiccup could not stop thinking about the Night Fury.
He secretly built it a new tail fin. When Hiccup finally
found the crippled dragon, he knew it would not be easy
fitting it with the new fin. But Hiccup was gentle and the
dragon began to trust him. He climbed onto the dragon's
back to test his handiwork.

'I did it!' Hiccup cheered as they flew through the sky.

Slowly the two enemies became friends. Hiccup
named the dragon Toothless.

Hiccup learned all sorts of dragon secrets from Toothless. He learned that dragons are ticklish and that they *really* hate eels!

Once at the Dragon Training Academy, Hiccup calmed an angry, two-headed Zippleback! Nobody saw Hiccup show the creature a yucky, stinky eel.

One day, a curious Astrid followed Hiccup after school.
'Don't be afraid,' Hiccup told her. 'Toothless won't hurt you.'
They climbed onto the dragon's back and went for a ride.
Suddenly, there were more dragons in the sky.
Hiccup, Astrid and Toothless followed them.
The dragons were taking the Vikings' food to their
leader, the Red Death!

When Stoick came to watch Hiccup's last battle, he thought his son was in danger. Stoick jumped in to battle the dragon himself. Just then, Toothless swooped into the ring and roared at the Viking chief.

Stoick charged towards Toothless.

'No!' Hiccup cried. 'Leave him alone!' Hiccup explained that the dragons were being forced to steal food for the Red Death.

Hiccup pleaded with Stoick to free Toothless, but Stoick would not listen. Hiccup went to the other kids.

'I need your help!' he told them. Then, he taught them each how to ride the other dragons.

The Red Death was like no dragon the
Vikings had ever seen before. He crushed
their weapons and destroyed their ships.
Then something incredible happened.
The Viking kids soared to the rescue!
Hiccup found Toothless and climbed
onto his back. They flew very close to the
enormous dragon's angry face.

The Red Death charged after Hiccup and Toothless.
Soon they found themselves in a perilous nosedive
headed straight for the ground below!

At the last second, Hiccup and Toothless pulled away.
But the giant dragon crashed into the ground at full speed!

Hiccup had tricked the terrible dragon. The Red
Death was gone for good!

Although Hiccup was hurt in the fight, he was a hero. Now the Vikings *and* dragons loved him.

'I'm proud to call you my son,' said Stoick.

Hiccup had saved the day and destroyed the worst dragon in the land. But best of all, he put the fighting between the Vikings of Berk and dragons to rest… forever!

Treasure Cove Stories

Book list may be subject to change.